LITTLE CRITTER®'S READ-IT-YOURSELF STORYBOOK

Six Funny Easy-to-Read Stories

BY MERCER MAYER

A GOLDEN BOOK • NEW YORK

Golden Books Publishing Company, Inc., New York, New York 10106

 Library of Congress Catalog Card Number: 92-73407 ISBN: 0-307-16840-9 10 9 8 7 6 5 4

FOREWORD

"Mom! Dad! Listen to me! I can read!" It's one of the most triumphant moments for any child—and any parent.

Now, of course, your new little reader wants to practice all the time. When children start reading, it takes time for their reading vocabulary to match their spoken vocabulary. They need books with easily recognizable words to encourage their sense of achievement. They need simple sentences because they can't yet keep track of complicated thoughts on paper—even though they may speak and understand long, complex sentences. And finally, children also need some words they don't know already to challenge them to further efforts. Stories with these elements draw children into reading independently.

Little Critter's Read-It-Yourself Storybook provides all these things. The vocabulary is carefully chosen and monitored to blend familiarity with challenge. Simple sentences, with a few complex ones mixed in, make reading easy and interesting for all children, whether they are getting ready to read, are beginning to read, or are already reading on their own.

Yet reading involves more than just words and sentences, and *Little Critter's Read-It-Yourself Storybook* is far more than that. Mercer Mayer's timeless characters and humorous situations come to life for children. Children will pick up this book over and over again to follow Little Critter's adventures. They'll laugh at Little Critter's escapades with his friends, his family, his pets, and much more.

Lively, interesting characters and situations, combined with ease of reading and a bit of challenge, are irresistible to young readers. Your child will return to these stories until every word has been mastered—and after that, too, for the pleasure and comfort of familiar old friends. In the end, that's what *Little Critter's Read-It-Yourself Storybook* will become: a beloved old friend.

Sally R. Bell
Reading Consultant

Contents

Little Critter's This Is My House

This is my house.
I live here.

My mom and dad
live here, too.

I have a dog.
I have a kitten.
They live in my house.

This is my little sister.
She lives here, too.

We eat in the kitchen.

We watch TV
in the family room.

Mom likes us
to play outside.

We have a swing.

We have a sandbox.

We have a tree house.

It is raining.
My little sister
should be inside now.

But the door
would not open, Mom.

We have stairs
in my house.

MY ROOM
KEEP OUT

The stairs go to
our bedrooms.
I have my own room.

My little sister
has her own room, too.

I have a car.

I have an airplane.

I have paints.

Sometimes I play games
with my little sister.

Sometimes I let her win.

Sometimes we play
other games.

Sometimes Mom gets mad.

We have a basement
in my house.

Sometimes I have to
put my things
down here.

I love my house.
I love my mom and dad.

And…
I love my little sister, too.

Little Critter's These Are My Pets

This is my frog.
He is green.

He likes to sit
in water.
I like to sit
in water.

He likes to hop.
I like to hop.

My frog is my friend.

This is my turtle.
He is green, too.

He likes to hide
in the grass.
I like to hide
in the grass.
My turtle is my friend.

This is my fish.
My fish is yellow.

She likes to swim.
I like to swim.

I like to look
at my fish.
My fish likes
to look at me.

My fish is my friend.

This is my dog.
My dog is brown and white.

My dog likes to run.
I like to run.

My dog likes to dig.
I like to dig.

My dog is my friend.

This is my kitten.
She is black and white.

She likes my dog.
She likes his tail
best of all.

My kitten likes
my frog, too.

My kitten likes
to sit in the sun.
I like to sit
in the sun.
My kitten is my friend.

This is my bug.
My bug is black.

My bug likes to fly.
I like to see
my bug fly.

My bug likes
to sit on my hand.

I keep my bug in a jar.
I like my bug.
My bug is my friend.

This is my snake.
My snake is green and yellow.

I keep my snake
in a cage.

My snake can move fast.
I can move fast.
My snake is my friend.

When I take a bath,
my friends want
to take a bath, too.
But Mom says, "No."

When I get in bed,
my friends get in bed, too.
But Mom says, “No.
No pets in bed.

"Just say good night
and go to sleep."

So my frog says good night.
My dog says good night.
My kitten says good night.

My other friends don't
say a thing.

I say good night
to my friends.
And we all go to sleep.

Little Critter's Little Sister's Birthday

It was my little sister's birthday.
We were going
to give her
a party.
She did not know that.

Dad and I went shopping.
My little sister wanted
to go, too.
But she had to stay home.

We were going
to get her
birthday present.
She did not know that.

Dad and I went
to the mall.
We were going
to the toy store.

CRITTER MALL
CRITTERVILLE'S
GOOD FOOD
DELI
TODA
SPECIA
CHE
$1.

This would be a good present.
But so would this.

Or this.
This would be a good present, too.

But so would this.
Or this.

But that would be
the best present.
For my little sister,
I mean.

We went home.
I put the present
in a box.
I got dressed.

I gave my little sister
her present.

The doorbell rang.
Surprise!
There were all of
my little sister's friends.

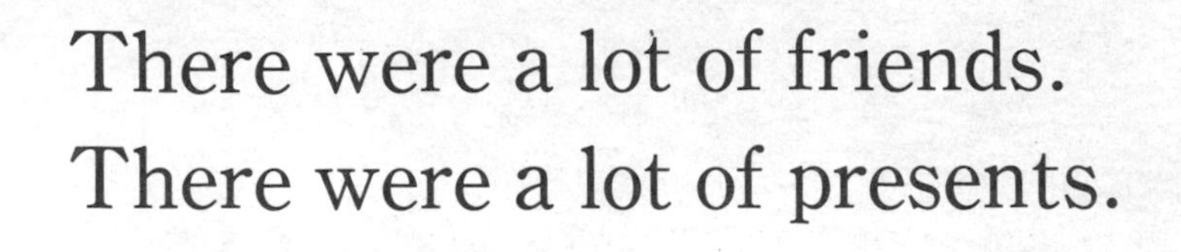

There were a lot of friends.
There were a lot of presents.

We went outside
to play games.
We had a bag race.

We had an egg race.

Then we went inside.
We played more games.

Mom brought out
the birthday cake.

My little sister
made a wish.
She blew out
all the candles.

Mom cut the cake.

There was a lot
of cake.

There was a piece
for everyone.

There was ice cream, too.

Then it was time
to open the presents.

My little sister
opened my present.
"Look at this!"
she cried.

She said it was
the best present.
I knew that.

Little Critter's
This Is My School

Today is my first day
of school.

I have new things
to wear.

I have a new pencil
and a notebook.

Mom gives me
money for lunch.

Mom gives me
an apple for
the teacher.

But I want
to give the teacher
my new bug.
Mom says an apple
is better.

Mom waits with me
for the school bus.

She does not have to wait,
because I am big.
But it makes her happy.

The bus is full.
The driver is quiet.
But we are not.
We are having fun.

CRITTERVILLE
LITTLE SCHOOL

I know where to go.
But I ask someone anyway.

My teacher is Miss Kitty.
I give her my apple.

Miss Kitty gives us
name tags.

I sit at my desk.
There are many kids
I do not know.

Everyone has to tell
something about himself.
I tell about going camping.
The bear took our food.

We learn a song.
Some kids do not sing.

We draw pictures.
I draw my family.

Then we go play outside.

After playtime Miss Kitty
reads a story.

The bell rings.
It is time for lunch.
I buy lunch
all by myself.

I sit with some
other kids.
We trade food.

After lunch we have
rest time.
I am not tired.
But I have to
lie down anyway.

After rest time
we go to the library.

We have the most books
in the world.

We meet the school nurse.

Then we see a film
about dinosaurs.
I am not scared.
Dinosaurs are all
dead anyway.

Then it is time
to go home.

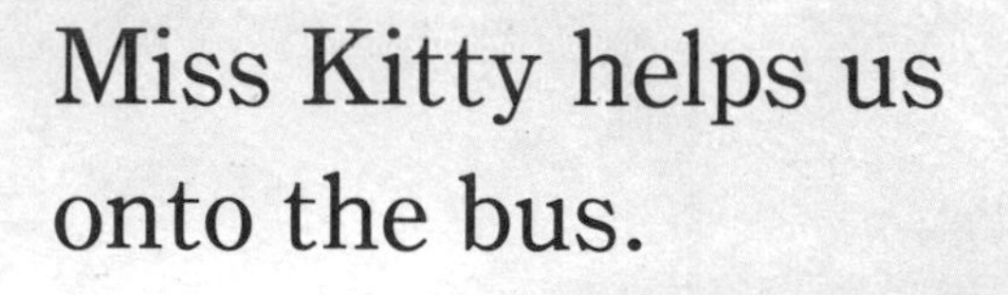

Miss Kitty helps us
onto the bus.

Tomorrow is show-and-tell.
I think I will bring
my pet snake.

Little Critter's This Is My Friend

This is my friend.
My friend is special.

I like to surprise my friend.

My friend and I talk
to each other
every day.

Sometimes my friend
does not like
what I say.

Sometimes I do not like
what my friend says.

Sometimes my friend
gives me things.
Today she gives me
a cookie.

I like cookies.
But this one is weird.

This cookie
is made of sand!
Yuck!

My friend thinks
this is funny.
I do not think
this is funny.

I try to tell
my friend that.
But my friend has
someplace to go.

Sometimes my friend
makes me mad.

Sometimes I make
my friend mad.

But I give her
some flowers.

My friend likes flowers.

Sometimes I fall down.
I hurt my arm!

My friend makes me
feel better.

A spider scares us.

But I am brave.
"Go away!
Do not scare my friend.
My friend is special,"
I say.

My friend shares with me.
That makes me happy.

I take a lick.
I take a bite.

I like ice cream.
It is so good.

My friend even
gives me the cone.

Sometimes I wait for
my friend.
I like to surprise my friend.

Sometimes I give
my friend things.
Now I give her
a present.

She opens the box.

"What is it?"
she asks.
"It is a rock,"
I say.
"It is my favorite rock."

"Thank you,"
says my friend.
She gives me a kiss.

My friend and I
give each other
many things.

But friendship is
the best there is.

Little Critter's Staying Overnight

I am going to sleep
at my friend's house.
His house is big.

Someone in funny clothes
opened the door.
There was my friend!

I said good-bye
to Mom.

Time to play!

We went
into the pool.

We played games
with balls.

We played tag.
We had a race.

We played
hide-and-seek.

Then we played
more games with balls.

Then we went inside.
My friend has
all of the
Bozo Builder Set.

He has a train
with lots of things.

His bear is big—
bigger than my bear.

But his dog
is small.
His dog is named
Froo-Froo.

It was time for dinner.
The napkin looked
like a hat.
I put it
on my head.

My friend has a TV
in his room.
We watched until
it was late.

It was time for bed.

We turned out
the lights.
It was dark—
a bigger dark
than in my room.

So I hugged my bear.

The next day
we played outside
again.

No, Froo-Froo!
Come back!

Stop, Froo-Froo!
Stop! Stop!

Got you!

It was a good time
to call Mom.

Thank you
for everything.
Bye-bye!

I had fun
at my friend's house.
But home is best.